**stick**

**linkage**

**little bucket**

To Chloe,
Sam and Harry,
with love
T.K.

For Karen
D.P.

First published 2018 by Walker Books Ltd, 87 Vauxhall Walk, London SE11 5HJ · Text © 2018 Timothy Knapman · Illustrations © 2018 Daron Parton The right of Timothy Knapman and Daron Parton to be identified as author and illustrator respectively of this work has been asserted by them in accordance with the Copyright, Designs and Patents Act 1988 · This book has been typeset in Futura · Printed in China · All rights reserved. No part of this book may be reproduced, transmitted or stored in an information retrieval system in any form or by any means, graphic, electronic or mechanical, including photocopying, taping and recording, without prior written permission from the publisher · British Library Cataloguing in Publication Data: a catalogue record for this book is available from the British Library · ISBN 978-1-4063-5583-3 www.walker.co.uk · 10 9 8 7 6 5 4 3 2 1

WALKER BOOKS
AND SUBSIDIARIES
LONDON · BOSTON · SYDNEY · AUCKLAND

# BIG DIGGER LITTLE DIGGER

**TIMOTHY KNAPMAN**          **DARON PARTON**

Little Digger lived on
a big building site.

**All the machines on the building site worked hard,
but Little Digger worked hardest of all.**

"Little Digger,

Little Digger,

**Little Digger loves to dig,"** said Little Digger,
as he dug holes all day long.

One day, Little Digger had an especially big hole to dig.
He wasn't sure he would be strong enough,
but he would try his best.

And he was just about to start, when ...

a new machine appeared!

**"Big Digger dig down DEEP,"** said Big Digger.

**And off he roared to work.**

**Now there was no hole for Little Digger to dig.**

He still wanted to be useful so he drove around
the building site looking for something to do.

But he couldn't dump like the dumper truck ...

**he couldn't mix like the cement mixer ...**

**he couldn't move things like the bulldozer ...**

and he kept getting in everyone's way.
**"Little Digger feels left out,"** said Little Digger.

Big Digger, meanwhile, was hard at work.
He dug the deepest hole
that anyone had EVER seen.
**"Big Digger dig down DEEP."**

In fact, it was SO deep,
that when Big Digger
tried to climb out,
he found that he couldn't!

"**Help!**" cried Big Digger.

Little Digger raced right over.

**"Big Digger dig down deep?
Little Digger get you out."**

Little Digger had an idea.
He rushed off and brought back
the dumper truck,
the cement mixer,
the bulldozer
and a very strong chain.

They all joined up together in a long line,
holding on tight to Little Digger.

At the edge of the deep, deep hole,
Little Digger stretched out with his little scoop.
And Big Digger stretched up with
his big scoop.

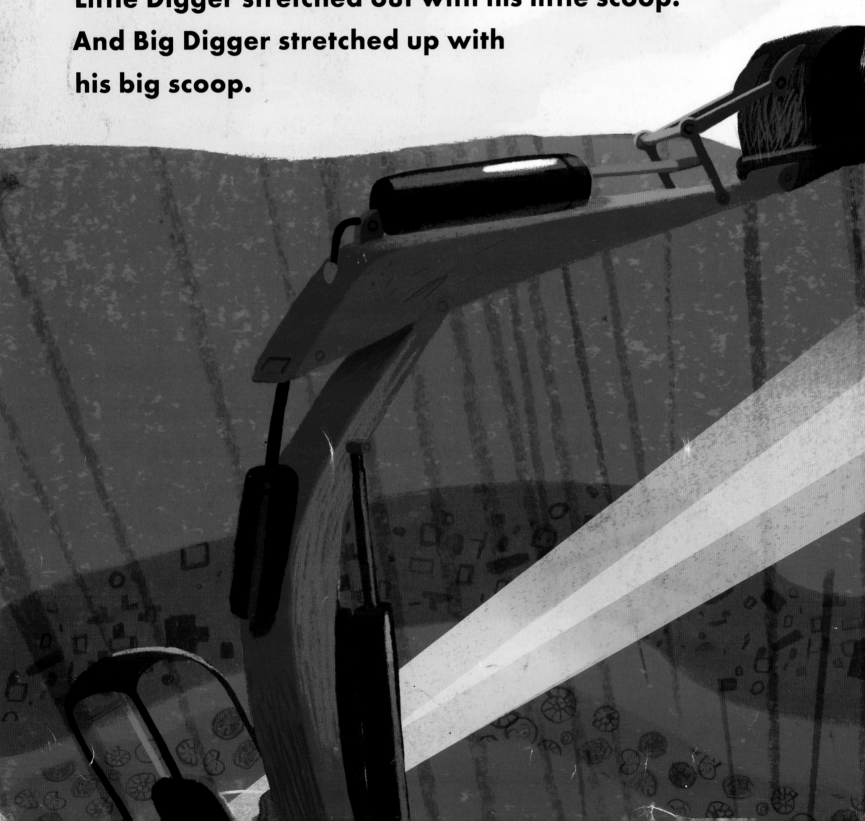

They touched ...
but only just.

Little Digger wasn't sure he would be
strong enough, but he would try his best.

**"Big Digger, Big Digger, Big Digger,"**
said Little Digger. And, locking scoops with Big Digger,
he pulled with all his might.

Big Digger was very, VERY heavy.
Little Digger felt his sprockets strain
and his bolts ache.

It couldn't work!

It WOULDN'T work!

**But then, at last ...**

Little Digger pulled Big Digger right out of the hole!

**"Little Digger, Little Digger, Little Digger!"**
said Big Digger.

And from that day on, Big Digger and Little Digger went everywhere together. Of all the machines on the building site, they worked the hardest.

"Big Digger, Little Digger,
Big Digger, Little Digger,"
said the diggers happily as
they dug holes all day long.

# BIG DIGGER

linkage

stick

big bucket